Presented to

_____

from

_____

_____

_____ 19 _____

Dear Parents:

Young children are interested in the world around them. To young children, that world may consist of only their own neighborhood and community. Follow Barney and his friends BJ™ and Baby Bop™ in their balloon ride over their community as they look for a lost puppy in BJ's care.

We consider books to be life-long gifts that develop and enhance the love of reading. We hope you enjoy reading along with Barney, Baby Bop and BJ!

Mary Ann Dudko, Ph.D.
Margie Larsen, M.Ed.
Early Childhood Educational Specialists

Art Director/Designer: Tricia Legault
©1995 The Lyons Group

PUBLISHING ®
A Division of The Lyons Group

300 East Bethany Drive, Allen, Texas 75002

6 7 8 9 10   97 96

ISBN 1-57064-044-0

Library of Congress Number 95-75347

Barney's Big Balloon

A Hide-and-Seek Adventure

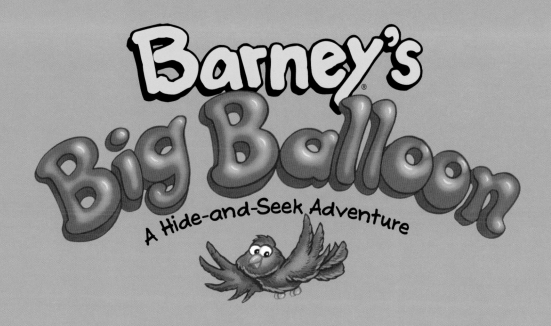

Written by Mark S. Bernthal
Illustrated by Chris Sharp and
David McGlothlin

BJ was having a wonderful day playing with a friend's puppy, Pepper. They had fun together all morning under the big tree in the backyard.

But later, BJ couldn't find the puppy anywhere. "Hmmmm," said Barney, "if we use our imaginations and put these sheets together, maybe we can fly up high and look for Pepper."

After sewing the sheets together, they huffed and puffed as hard as they could. The balloon grew bigger . . . and bigger . . . and bigger!

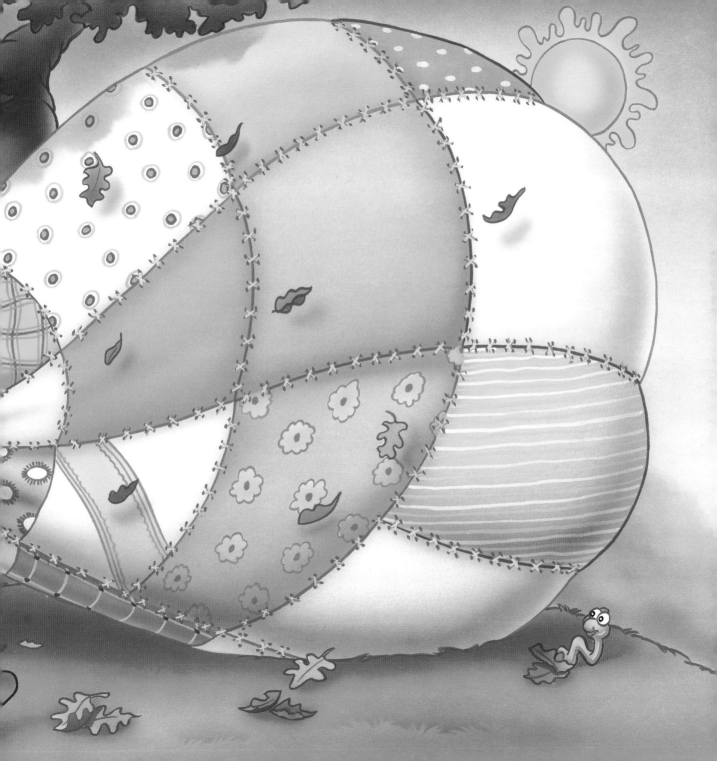

Soon Barney's big balloon climbed high into the sky! "That cloud looks just like a turtle," said Baby Bop.

BJ looked for the lost puppy. "Aye yie yie! What *will* I do? I don't see Pepper. How about you?"

Baby Bop saw a big red fire truck and a little green car in the neighborhood. "Over there, BJ," said Baby Bop. "Is that the puppy in the tree? No, that is a cat."

"Patti's riding her bike!" said Barney. But the puppy was nowhere in sight.

BJ was worried. "Aye yie yie! What *will* I do? I don't see Pepper. How about you?"

Barney loved seeing the tall buildings downtown. "Beep! Beep!" went a yellow taxi.

But BJ still didn't see the puppy. "Aye yie yie! What *will* I do? I don't see Pepper. How about you?"

Barney's big balloon floated up over the school.
"There's the school bus," shouted Baby Bop,
"and look! The children are out playing."

BJ looked for the puppy. "Aye yie yie!
What *will* I do? I don't see Pepper.
How about you?"

"Look, BJ," shouted Baby Bop, "cows and horses and pigs!"

"Cock-a-doodle-doo, Mr. Rooster!" crowed Barney.

But BJ said, "Aye yie yie! What *will* I do? I don't see Pepper. How about you?"

Barney flew his big balloon back
to the yard.

Suddenly BJ shouted happily,
"Aye yie yie! Look what I see!
It's Pepper the puppy
under the tree!"

BJ was so happy. "Pepper wasn't lost after all!" he said. "She was hiding under the leaves all the time!"

BJ said, "Pepper the puppy is safe by my side."

"And we had a very nice big balloon ride!" laughed Barney.